This book belongs to

Franklin's Classic Treasury
Volume II

Franklin is a trade mark of Kids Can Press Ltd.

Franklin's Classic Treasury, Volume II
© 2000 by P.B. Creations Inc. and Brenda Clark Illustrator Inc.

This book includes the following stories:
Franklin Is Lost first published in 1992
Franklin Wants a Pet first published in 1995
Franklin's Blanket first published in 1995
Franklin and the Tooth Fairy first published in 1995

All text copyright © 1992, 1995 by P.B. Creations Inc.
All illustrations copyright © 1992, 1995
by Brenda Clark Illustrator Inc.

Kids Can Press acknowledges the financial support of the Ontario Arts Council, the Canada Council for the Arts and the Government of Canada, through the BPIDP, for our publishing activity. **Canadä**

Published in Canada by	Published in the U.S. by
Kids Can Press Ltd.	Kids Can Press Ltd.
29 Birch Avenue	4500 Witmer Industrial Estates
Toronto, ON M4V 1E2	Niagara Falls, NY 14305–1386

Printed in Hong Kong by Wing King Tong Co. Ltd.

CM 00 0 9 8 7 6 5 4 3 2 1

Canadian Cataloguing in Publication Data

Bourgeois, Paulette
      Franklin's classic treasury

Contents: [v. I] Franklin in the dark. Hurry up Franklin. Franklin fibs. Franklin is bossy. – [v. II] Franklin is lost. Franklin wants a pet. Franklin's blanket. Franklin and the tooth fairy.

ISBN 1-55074-742-8 (v. I)   ISBN 1-55074-813-0 (v. II)

I. Clark, Brenda. II. Title.

PS8553.O85477F85   2000   jC813'.54   C99-930503-4
PZ7.B6654Fr 1999

Kids Can Press is a Nelvana company

❧ Franklin's ❧

CLASSIC

Treasury

Volume II

Paulette Bourgeois • Brenda Clark

Kids Can Press

Contents

Franklin Is Lost

Written by Paulette Bourgeois
Illustrated by Brenda Clark

FRANKLIN could slide down a river bank. He could count forwards and backwards. He could zip zippers and button buttons. He could even walk to Bear's house all by himself. But Franklin was not allowed to go into the woods alone.

One day Franklin said, "I'm going to play at Bear's house."

"All right," said Franklin's mother. "But be home for dinner by six o'clock." She showed him the time with the hands of the clock. "And Franklin," she warned, "don't go into the woods alone."

13

Franklin raced down the path, over the bridge and across the berry patch.

Bear was there. Fox was there. Goose and Otter were there.

"I'm here," huffed Franklin. "What are you playing?"

"Hide and seek," shouted his friends. "And you're It."

Franklin started counting. Hide and seek was his favourite game. He wasn't very fast but he was very clever. He knew Bear always hid in the berry patch.

Franklin looked around. He saw a shaggy paw swipe at a branch of berries.

"I see you, Bear," he called.

Franklin spotted feathers and fur under the bridge.
"I see you, Goose. I see you, Otter," he called.

Only Fox was left to find. Franklin walked this way and that. He looked into bushes and searched under logs. He walked along the path and over the bridge and without even thinking, he walked right into the woods.

He looked into burrows and all around trees. Franklin searched everywhere but he couldn't find Fox.

Fox wasn't in the woods at all. He was hiding inside Bear's house. After awhile he shouted, "Can't catch me!"

But Franklin couldn't hear him. He was too far away.

"Where's Franklin?" asked Fox.

Nobody knew.

They waited a long time. Bear's tummy grumbled. Finally, Goose said, "It's almost six o'clock. Franklin must have hurried home for supper."

"Of course," they said, and off they went.

At Franklin's house, the clock struck six. Franklin's parents were annoyed. Their supper was ready.

By half-past six, they were worried and went looking for Franklin.

Franklin's father searched along the path. "Franklin," he called. "Where are you?"

Franklin's mother talked to his friends.
"Where's Franklin?" she asked Bear.

"Where's Franklin?" she asked Otter and Goose.
"Where's Franklin?" she asked Fox.
Nobody knew. Now they were worried, too.

It was getting dark. Franklin turned one way and then another. Every tree looked the same. Every rock looked the same. He couldn't find the path.

"I'm lost," said Franklin in a tiny little voice.

He couldn't remember which way he had come. He didn't know which way to go. He was tired and frightened and all alone. Franklin curled up in his small dark shell and waited. Somebody would come. Sometime. Wouldn't they?

Dark shadows flitted across the rocks.

"Who's there?" whispered Franklin. But no one answered because it was the clouds blowing across the face of the moon.

"Whoo. Whoo."

"Who's there?" whispered Franklin. But no one answered because it was Owl far, far away.

"Whewwww. Whewwww."

"Who's there?" whispered Franklin. But no one answered because it was the wind whistling through the trees.

Franklin tried to sleep, but every sound made him jump.

He was humming himself a little tune when he heard: "Crick, crack, crick, crack, crick, crack, squish."

"Who's there?" whispered Franklin. But no one answered.

Then Franklin heard a new sound. It sounded like someone calling his name.

He heard it again.

"Here I am! Here I am!" Franklin shouted over and over.

CRICK CRACK, CRICK CRACK, CRICK CRACK, SQUISH. Franklin's parents came over the knoll.

"There you are!" They hugged him and kissed him and held him tight.

"We were so worried," said Franklin's father.

"You were told not to go into the woods alone," scolded his mother.

"It wasn't on purpose," sniffled Franklin. "I was looking for Fox and I forgot."

"Well, thank goodness you're safe," said Franklin's parents.

They found the path and walked all the way home. Their supper was still warm in the oven. After two helpings of everything, Franklin had something important to say.

"I'm sorry. I promise I'll never go into the woods alone again."

"Even if Fox hides there?" asked his mother.

"Even if Bear hides there?" asked his father.

"Even if everybody hides there!" said Franklin.

It was half-past bedtime. Franklin crawled into his warm, safe shell.

"Good night, dear," said his parents.
But no one answered because Franklin
had fallen fast asleep.

Franklin Wants a Pet

Written by Paulette Bourgeois
Illustrated by Brenda Clark

FRANKLIN could count by twos and tie his shoes.
He could sleep alone in his small, dark shell. He even
had a best friend named Bear. But Franklin wanted
something else. He wanted a pet.

Franklin had wanted a pet since he was small. But whenever he asked, "May I have a pet, please?" his parents said, "Maybe someday."

Franklin waited for a long time. He often pretended to have a pet. He took Sam, his stuffed dog, for walks. He taught Sam tricks. He even helped Sam bury some bones.
But Sam wasn't a real pet.

One day, Franklin asked his parents again, "May I have a pet, please?"

Franklin's parents looked at each other.

"We'll think about it," they answered.

At first, Franklin was happy because they did not say, *No*. Then, Franklin became worried. His parents could think about things for days and days.

That day, Franklin visited Bear and told him all about the pet he wanted.

"If I had a pet, it would be a bird," said Bear.

"Why?" asked Franklin.

"Because birds sing beautiful songs," said Bear.

"Birds are nice," said Franklin. "But their loud singing may wake me too early."

Franklin waited until morning before asking his parents if they had finished thinking yet.

"Not quite," said Franklin's mother. "We need to know that you could care for a pet."

Franklin nodded his head up and down.

"Could you feed your pet?" asked Franklin's father.

Franklin nodded again. He almost said please one hundred times in a row but he stopped himself.

Franklin visited Beaver and told her all about the pet he wanted.

"If I had a pet it would be a cat," said Beaver.

"Why?" asked Franklin.

"Because cats make purring sounds," she answered.

"Cats are nice," said Franklin. "But you never know where they are."

Later that day, Franklin asked his parents, "Are you finished thinking?"

"Not yet," they answered.

"Please hurry," said Franklin.

His father sighed. "Franklin, this is a big decision. A pet costs money to buy and to keep."

Franklin offered all the money in his piggy bank and hoped it was enough.

After counting his pennies, Franklin visited with Goose and told her all about the pet he wanted.

"If I had a pet, it would be a bunny," said Goose.

"Why?" asked Franklin.

"Because bunnies have wiggly whiskers."

"Bunnies are nice," said Franklin. "But I think whiskers might make me sneeze."

After three whole days, Franklin was tired of waiting for his parents to finish thinking. He had a plan!

He brought Sam to the breakfast table. "I have been taking care of Sam for a long, long time," he said. "I will take good care of a real pet, too. I will feed it. I will clean its house. We can take it to the vet if it gets sick."

Franklin's parents smiled. "It sounds as if you've been doing a lot of thinking, too," they said.

"So may I have a pet, please?" he begged.

They whispered to each other. Then they nodded their heads up and down.

"Oh, thank you," said Franklin. He wanted to go to the pet store right away.

"We'll help you choose a puppy tomorrow," said his father.

"No thank you," said Franklin. "I do not want a dog."
His parents were surprised.
"Dogs are nice," said Franklin. "But I want a quiet pet."
Franklin's mother asked if he wanted a kitten.
"No thank you," said Franklin. "Kittens are nice but
I want a pet that stays close by."

"Is it a hamster that you want?" said Franklin's father.

Franklin shook his head. "No thank you."

"A rabbit?" asked Franklin's mother.

"No thank you," said Franklin.

"What kind of pet do you want?" asked his parents.

Franklin smiled and said, "I'll show you tomorrow."

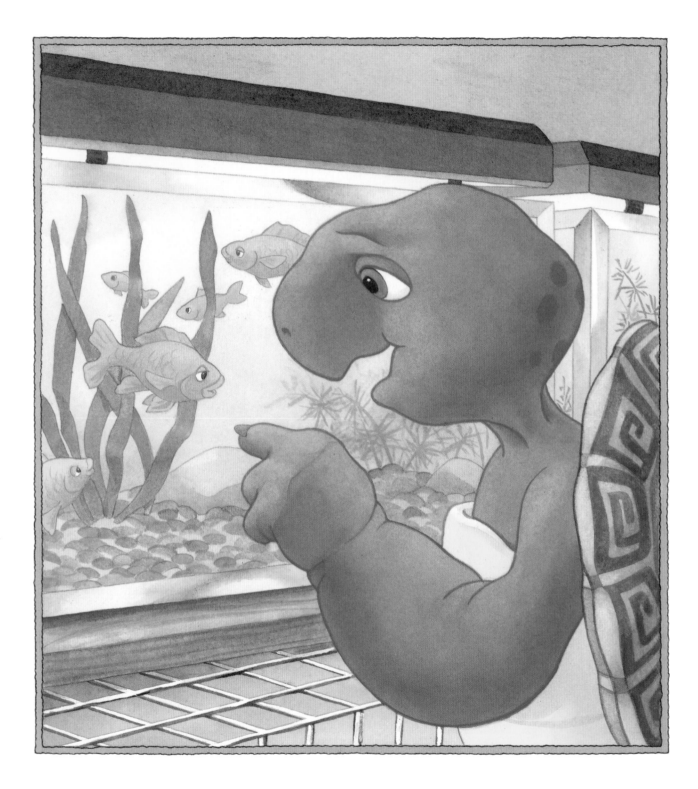

At the pet store, Franklin pointed to a fish.

"I want a goldfish," he said.

"A goldfish!" they said. "Why? A fish cannot do tricks or play with you."

So Franklin explained. He liked to watch fish swim slowly around and around. He liked their beautiful colours. And he liked the way they made him feel inside. Quiet and calm.

"Besides," he said. "I love goldfish."

"That's the best reason of all," said Franklin's parents.

Franklin named his fish Goldie. He took very good care of her, just as he'd promised.

Every morning, Franklin watched Goldie swim around and around. And every night before he went to bed, Franklin blew a great, big fish kiss and whispered, "I love you, Goldie."

Franklin's Blanket

Written by Paulette Bourgeois
Illustrated by Brenda Clark

FRANKLIN could slide down a riverbank all by himself. He could count by twos and tie his shoes. He could even sleep alone — as long as he had a goodnight story, a goodnight hug, a glass of water, a night light and his blue blanket.

71

In the beginning, the blanket was big and soft and edged in satin. But with all the snuggling and cuddling, it now had holes in the middle and tatters along the edges. Every year, as Franklin got bigger, his blue blanket got smaller.

Franklin usually kept his blanket folded in his top drawer. One night it wasn't there. Franklin searched around his room. He rummaged through his toy chest. He took everything out of his drawers and his books off the shelves. But he could not find his blue blanket anywhere.

He ran to tell his parents.

"Go back to bed," they said as soon as they saw him.

"But, but … " said Franklin.

"No buts," said Franklin's father. "You have had a goodnight story, a goodnight hug, two glasses of water, and I turned on your night light myself."

"But I can't find my blanket," said Franklin.

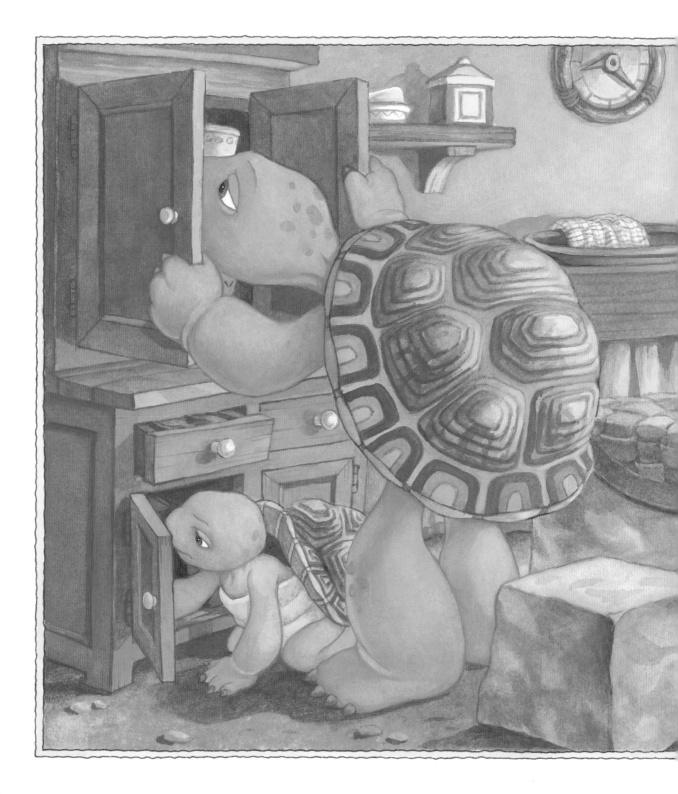

So Franklin and his parents hunted everywhere.
"Try to remember," said Franklin's mother. "When did you last have it?"

Franklin thought.

In the morning, after a fight with Bear, Franklin had snuggled with the blanket until he felt better.

In the afternoon, when thunder crashed and lightning flashed, Franklin had covered himself with the blanket until all was calm.

He was sure that after the storm he had put the blanket back where it belonged.

When Franklin and his parents looked, the blanket wasn't there.

"We'll find it tomorrow," said Franklin's mother.

"I can't sleep without my blanket," said Franklin.

"I have an idea," said Franklin's father. He left the room and came back with an old, yellow blanket.

"What's that?" asked Franklin.

"It was mine," said Franklin's father. "Maybe it will make you feel better."

Franklin tried to snuggle the old, yellow blanket, but it wasn't the same. He missed his own blanket terribly, and it took Franklin a long, long time to fall asleep.

The next morning Franklin began a search for his blanket. He went to Bear's house first. He looked so glum that Bear asked, "What's wrong, Franklin? Did your mother give you brussels sprouts again?"

"Worse," said Franklin. "I can't find my blanket."

"It's not here," said Bear. "Besides, my mother says big bears like me are too old for baby blankets. Maybe you don't need a blanket."

Franklin knew that Bear always slept with his stuffed bunny. "What about your bunny?" asked Franklin.

"Bunnies are different," said Bear.

Next he tried Fox's house. The blanket wasn't there either.

"Why don't we play?" asked Fox.

"No," said Franklin. "I want to find my blanket."

"My father says worn-out blankets are no good to anybody," said Fox. "Maybe you should get a new blanket. I did."

"I like my old blanket," said Franklin.

Then Franklin went to Beaver's house. The blanket wasn't there. Franklin looked so sad that Beaver said, "You can borrow my Teddy until you find your blanket."

"Thank you, Beaver," said Franklin, holding Teddy tightly.

That night when Franklin went to bed, he had his father's yellow blanket and Beaver's Teddy. But it wasn't the same as sleeping with his own blue blanket.

At breakfast, Franklin's father sniffed and pinched his nose. "Do you smell something odd?" he asked. "A sort of musty, old-sock smell?"

Franklin and his mother sniffed, too.

Then Franklin remembered. "I think I know what smells," he said.

Franklin reached under his chair and pulled out his blue blanket. Plop! A handful of cold, slimy brussels sprouts spilled out of the blanket and onto the floor.

His mother and father stared with amazement.

"Look!" said Franklin. "I found my blanket. I forgot I put it here."

"You forgot to eat your brussels sprouts, too," said Franklin's mother.

"Whoops," said Franklin, looking a little sheepish.

"Old, cold brussels sprouts sure do stink," said Franklin's father.

"All brussels sprouts stink," said Franklin.

Franklin's mother smiled. "I used to hate cabbage," she said. "Now *that's* a stinky vegetable."

"Asparagus!" said Franklin's father. "That's even stinkier than brussels sprouts and cabbage mixed together."

"Broccoli!" shouted Franklin. Then he stopped. He liked broccoli. "It stinks, but I wouldn't hide broccoli," he said.

"That's good news," said his father.

Franklin helped to tidy the mess.

Then Franklin picked up his blanket.
"I don't care that you are old and full of holes,"
he said. "But you sure do need a bath."

That night, before his goodnight story, his goodnight hug and a glass of water, Franklin put his father's yellow blanket back where it belonged. He was glad he lived in a house where even old blankets had their special place.

Franklin and
the Tooth Fairy

Written by Paulette Bourgeois
Illustrated by Brenda Clark

FRANKLIN could count by twos and tie his shoes. He had lots of good friends, and one best friend, named Bear. Franklin and Bear were the same age. They lived in the same neighbourhood. They liked the same games. But one morning, Franklin discovered a way that he and Bear were different.

Waiting for the school bus, Bear put his paw in his mouth and wiggled a tooth back and forth. It jiggled and wiggled and then, with a tug, it came out.

"Look at this!" said Bear. "I lost my first tooth."

Franklin was startled. There was even a little blood on the tooth. "That's terrible. How are you going to tell your mother?"

Bear laughed.

103

"My teeth are supposed to fall out," said Bear. "It makes room for my grown-up teeth."

Franklin ran his tongue around his gums. They were smooth and firm ... and completely toothless.

"I don't have any teeth," said Franklin.

It was Bear's turn to be surprised.

Franklin's friends shook their heads sadly. "Too bad," they said.

Franklin wondered why. He had never needed teeth before.

Bear wrapped his tooth in a bit of tissue and put it in his backpack. "I need to keep this safe," he said.

108

All the way to school, Franklin wondered why Bear
wanted to keep his old tooth. Especially if he was
going to get a brand-new grown-up tooth. Now *that*
was exciting.

"Why do you want to keep your tooth?" asked
Franklin. "Won't you get a big one soon?"

All his friends looked at him with amazement.

"Don't you know about the tooth fairy?" asked Fox. Franklin shook his head.

"At night, before you go to sleep, you put your baby tooth under your pillow. Then the tooth fairy comes and takes the tooth away," explained Fox.

"But that's stealing," said Franklin. "Besides, what does the tooth fairy do with all those teeth?"

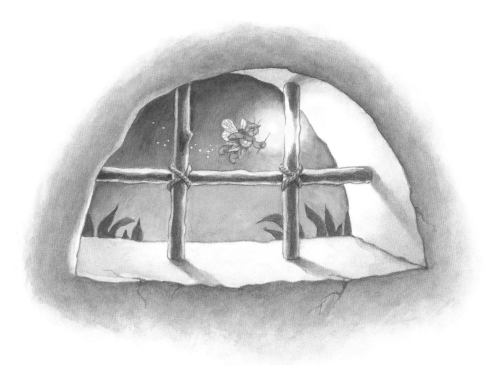

112

There was a long pause.

Bear scratched his head. Fox swished his tail, and Rabbit twitched.

"I don't know," said Bear, "but she always leaves something behind."

"One of her own teeth?" asked Franklin.

Everybody laughed.

"Oh, Franklin!" said Fox. "The tooth fairy leaves a present."

Franklin wondered what kind of present a tooth fairy would leave.

"I hope I get some money," said Bear.

"When I lost my first tooth, I got a new book," said Raccoon.

"I got crayons," Fox said.

Franklin rubbed his gums. He wished he had a tooth to leave for the tooth fairy. He wanted a present, too.

Bear showed his tooth to Mr. Owl as soon as he got to school.

Mr. Owl was very excited. "Losing your baby teeth means you are growing up," he said.

Franklin did not say anything. He had no teeth, but he wanted to feel grown-up, too.

Franklin was quiet for the rest of the day.

Even at home, Franklin was quieter than usual.

"What's wrong?" asked Franklin's mother.

"I don't have any teeth," he answered.

"Neither do we," said his father. "That's the way turtles are."

"But I want teeth," said Franklin. His parents looked surprised.

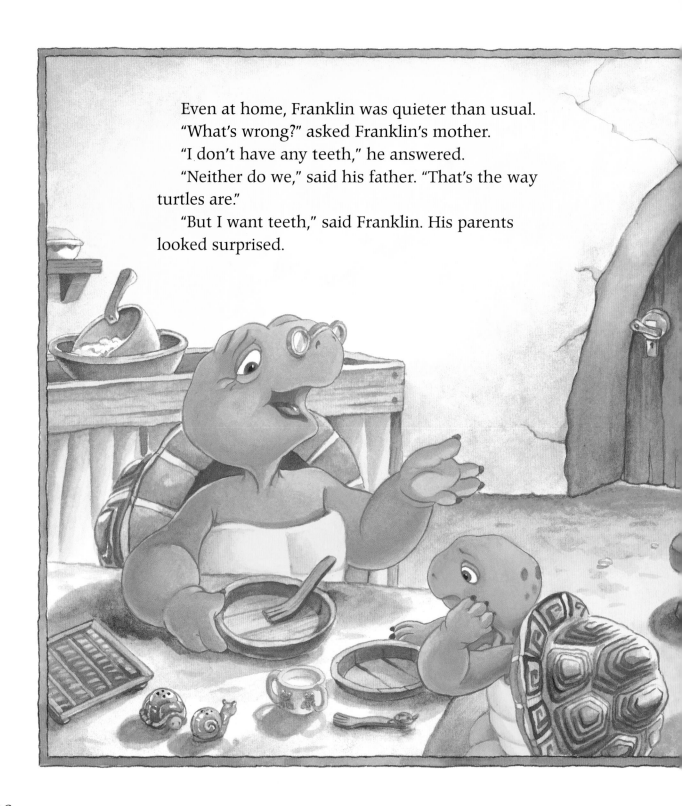

"My friends get presents from the tooth fairy when they lose their teeth," said Franklin.

"Why do they get presents for old teeth?" asked Franklin's father.

"Because it means they are growing up," said Franklin.

"I see," said his father.

121

That night, just before bed, Franklin had a good idea. Perhaps tooth fairies did not know that turtles have no teeth. He found a tiny white rock to put under his shell.

He asked his mother to help him write a note. It read:

Dear Tooth Fairy,

This is a turtle tooth. You may not have seen one before. Please leave a present.

Franklin

Franklin woke up very early the next morning. He looked under his shell. The rock was gone, but there was a note instead of a present.

He ran to his parents' room. "What does it say?" he asked.

Franklin's father put on his reading glasses.

Dear Franklin,

Sorry. Turtles don't have teeth.
Good try.

Your friend, The Tooth Fairy

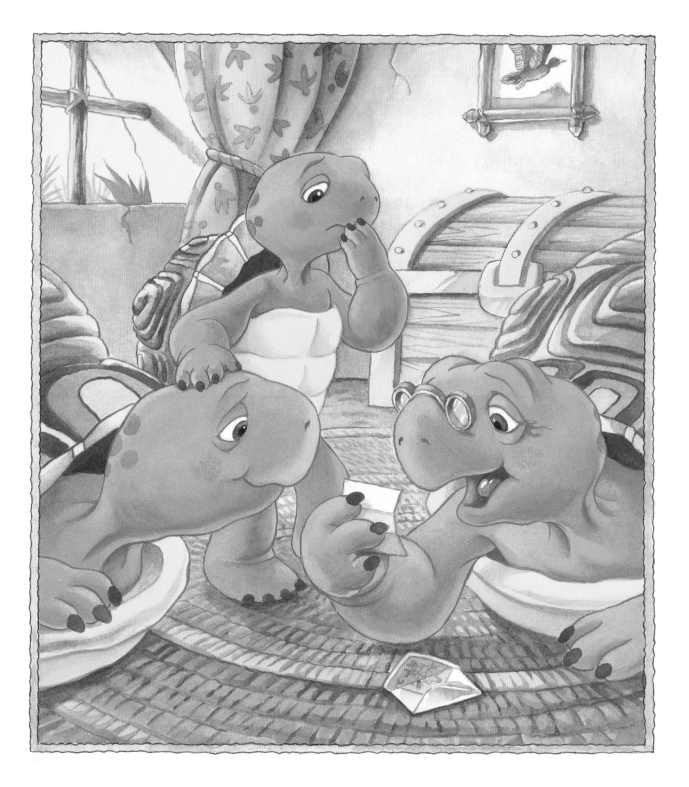

Franklin was very unhappy until he noticed a big wrapped package near his breakfast bowl.

"Open it," said Franklin's mother.

Inside was a beautiful book.

"Who is it from?" asked Franklin.

"From us," said his parents. "To celebrate your growing up."

Franklin stood very tall. "Thank you."

From then on, Franklin didn't worry about being different from Bear. He knew that, in all the important ways, he and Bear were exactly the same.